Dear Kathryn + Keith

Thought you might enjoy this reference manual as you venture into your new life experiences.

Mary Ann Bogie
Sept 1994

KATE GREENAWAY'S
MOTHER GOOSE

KATE GREENAWAY'S
MOTHER GOOSE

or Old Nursery Rhymes

The Complete Facsimile Sketchbooks

From the Arents Collections, The New York Public Library

Foreword by Bernard McTigue

Introduction by Rodney Engen

HARRY N. ABRAMS, INC.,
PUBLISHERS, NEW YORK

Kate Greenaway's Mother Goose was first published in
London in 1881. The Mother Goose rhymes accompanying
Kate Greenaway's sketchbook pages were taken from the
first printed edition of her book.

Project Director: Darlene Geis
Designer: Samuel N. Antupit

Library of Congress Cataloging-in-Publication Data

Mother Goose.
    Mother Goose, or, the old nursery rhymes /
illustrated by Kate Greenaway.
        p.   cm.
    Facsimile pages from Greenaway's sketchbooks
in the Arents Collections, the New York Public Library.
    Summary: A collection of traditional nursery
rhymes with watercolor illustrations.
Includes a history of Kate Greenaway's sketchbooks and of
her art in general.
    ISBN 0–8109–1031–4
    1. Nursery rhymes. 2. Children's poetry.
[1. Nursery rhymes.]
I. Greenaway, Kate, 1846–1901, ill. II. Title.
III. Title: Old Nursery rhymes.
PZ8.3.M85 1988d
398'.8—dc19   88–3411
                                   CIP
                                   AC

A Times Mirror Company

Printed and bound in Japan

CONTENTS

KATE GREENAWAY
IN THE ARENTS COLLECTIONS

George Arents acquired Kate Greenaway's manuscript of *Mother Goose or the Old Nursery Rhymes* in September 1954. He bought it at auction at Sotheby's, London, paying £1,500 (about $7,500 at 1954 exchange rates, about $40,000 in current dollar values) for the two little linen-covered sketchbooks in which Kate's original title was *Nursery Rhymes for Children*. In the first edition the title became *Mother Goose or the Old Nursery Rhymes*. Later the same year he gave the manuscript to The New York Public Library to join the collections he had been donating to The Library since 1943.

These collections, housed in their own pine-panelled rooms on The Library's third floor, reflect Mr. Arents' two main collecting interests: the history of tobacco, and books in parts and associated literature. The *Mother Goose* manuscript joined the latter collection, where it was to be in company with a fine group of nineteenth-century English literary works and illustrated books. Among these is a complete set of the children's books illustrated by Randolph Caldecott, a contemporary of Greenaway, together with the original drawings for his *Ride a Cock Horse to Banbury Cross*. In the neighboring tobacco collection the manuscript is together with other children's classics such as first editions of *Huckleberry Finn*, *Alice in Wonderland*, and the inscribed copy of *The Wizard of Oz*, which L. Frank Baum had presented to his mother. (These books merit inclusion in the tobacco collection because in each of them someone smokes something!)

In making a gift of his collections to The Library, Mr. Arents, a native New Yorker, was not only engaging in an act of civic virtue, he was also placing his holdings in an institution where they fit in perfectly well with those given by other donors over the past 150 years. He knew of The Library's strong interest in American history, English literature, and book illustration, and he knew his collections would be appreciated and utilized by the audience The Library attracted. He also knew of The Library's great collections of children's literature and of its pioneering work in providing books for the enjoyment of the children of New York City.

But the Greenaway manuscript, although illustrated and written as a children's book, was not to be handled by children. Its fragility and rarity dictated that it be used only by scholars under the strictest supervision.

With this first facsimile of *Mother Goose*, Mr. Arents' generous gift and Kate Greenaway's charming art may now be shared with everyone.

The facsimile pages should come as some surprise to those who think that they know Kate Greenaway's work through the printed editions of her books. *Mother Goose* is, in fact, a finer work of art than the printed illustrations, even those in the first edition, suggest. What becomes clear in comparing the original watercolors with their printed versions is Greenaway's delight in pale and vibrant color contrasts, which she employed to vivify her simple tableaus. Here, perhaps for the first time, one can see that Kate Greenaway's abilities were not merely decorative but also artistic. Her blues and greens shimmer across the tiny pages, and her yellows positively vibrate. In the early printed versions of these images, produced according to the technological limitations of the times, there is little hint of this vibrancy. The colors in the first edition are more muted, flatter, duller than her original illustrations in these sketchbooks would indicate. Attention is focused on the sweetness of the imagery, the visions of domestic and bucolic calm with which she is generally associated rather than on the vivacity and vigor of her art.

That Kate Greenaway wished to share this private vision of her work is evident from the fact that in 1882, a year after her *Mother Goose* was published, she gave the manuscript to her friend, Frederick Locker, who in turn bequeathed it to his daughter. In a letter written on June 18, 1941, his daughter (then Mrs. Morgan) wrote of her "precious Kate Greenaway." She had been forced to sell the manuscript in order to obtain money to help a needy relative. She writes to the new owner with the "hope your grandchild will appreciate it some day," and of Kate Greenaway as "an enchanting companion." She closes her letter with the note that "it is a pity for them to hide their beauty in the little morocco case."

Although the morocco case is long gone, replaced by a utilitarian, buckram-covered box, the pity of hiding them away remained evident to The Library's staff. It is to be hoped that through this facsimile many people will be able to enjoy these little books, while the originals, which they so carefully replicate, remain to be treasured by posterity.

Bernard McTigue
Curator, The Arents Collections

KATE GREENAWAY
AND MOTHER GOOSE

Rodney Engen

The story of Kate Greenaway's rise to fame and fortune reads like the finest children's fairy tale, a Victorian Cinderella story in which the promise of wealth and fame is the reward for years of silent drudgery. A shy, reserved child born on March 17, 1846, and brought up in the grim back streets of London's East End, Kate Greenaway was the daughter of a dedicated wood engraver father and an independent-minded mother. An escapist by nature, Kate (or Catherine as she was christened) spent her childhood in a series of cramped neighborhoods in Hackney and Islington, her restrictive fear of city life relieved only during long visits to her mother's relatives in the idyllic countryside of Nottinghamshire. It was here young Kate learned to dream, to stretch her imagination, and to hope for a better life than she saw in the struggles of her parents to survive in London. There she watched her father often drive himself throughout the night to finish an engraving for the popular press, and she determined to work hard to improve their future.

John Greenaway had been impoverished by the bankruptcy of a publisher for whom he had engraved illustrations for a Dickens publication. Months of work for which he received no pay caused him and his young family to abandon their lives together temporarily, Mrs. Greenaway taking young Kate and her brother into the country while her husband attempted to restore his fortunes. Greenaway remained a respected wood engraver for over thirty years, but he and his family would never truly recover from the disaster. When Kate was about six, Mrs. Greenaway opened a fancy goods store in London (where she taught her daughter dressmaking) to help support the family; much later the financial burdens were to fall upon the young girl.

Art school beckoned when Kate was twelve, and for over eleven years she attended classes regularly, a devoted student with the drive to succeed. From her local art school she graduated to the more prestigious National Art Training School at South Kensington, later called the Royal College of Art, where students endured a series of painstakingly tedious lessons as copyists, first from geometric designs suitable for commercial decorative objects such as tiles and carpets, then from plaster casts, and finally from objects in nature. Kate won medals for her work in 1861, 1864, and 1869, while aware that her more talented and ambitious fellow students with fine art aspirations soon turned elsewhere for training. Eventually, she, too, enrolled in evening classes at the pioneering Slade School, where women and men were allowed to study from the live model together, free from restriction and prejudice. Her spare time was spent perfecting watercolors and drawings of fantasy creatures to exhibit in the London galleries.

Ready at last to try to earn some money from her work, Kate brought a selection of pieces to The Dudley Gallery in Piccadilly. She was overjoyed when a watercolor and several drawings of gnomes and fairy creatures were chosen for one of the gallery's shows. The work attracted some interest, and her first patron, Reverend W.J. Loftie, editor of *People's Magazine*, who published her first fairy drawings.

About this time Kate's freelance career was launched when, thanks to the gallery, Reverend Loftie, and Kate's father's connections, she accepted some commercial design assignments from the greeting card firm of Marcus Ward & Co. as well as commissions for occasional black-and-white illustrations from magazines and children's book publishers.

As a young freelance illustrator Kate Greenaway accepted the rigors of deadlines and the seemingly ephemeral nature of magazine work; if anything, the experience helped to nurture her exalted ambitions of painting for the prestigious London galleries. She was prolific, and the number of greeting card designs she produced for Marcus Ward alone amounted to about 150–200 over a ten year period. She worked in a small backstreet studio room down an alleyway in Islington, not far from her mother's shop. Here she began to paint watercolor portraits of the local street urchins, a violet or a watercress vender who had attracted her with appropriately innocent expressions, and these children she dressed in costumes of her own design—mostly pastiches of the Regency doll clothes she had played with in the country, or variations on the popular Pre-Raphaelite medievalism of floral brocades and heavy gowns. Some of these child portraits found their way onto Marcus Ward greeting cards as well and proved so successful that they were reissued as colorplates in Ward gift books.

By 1877 Kate had managed to secure a steady income from such freelance commercial hackwork and had her first picture accepted for hanging at the prestigious Royal Academy. It was an auspicious start for the year, proving that she was well on the way to becoming a competent commercial artist. However, she retained some of her mother's independence and despite the pleas from her father that she must remain satisfied with her achievements, she nurtured loftier, more personal ambitions. It was a long-standing dream to have a book of her own illustrations and verses published, and throughout the year she labored over just such a project. The manuscript was accepted for publication, and this sixty-four page book of wood-engraved color illustrations was to become one of the most commercially successful children's books of the period.

Under the Window was, in fact, a curious mixture of childish fantasy, historical escapism, and improbable yet charmingly naive verses, each page designed and illustrated by the artist in her distinctively idealized style. Kate dressed her young characters in quaint shepherd's smocks and long pastel-tinted gowns, and she paraded them around the book's cover against an "Aesthetic" green which struck a welcome note with members of the tastemaking Aesthetic Movement. In an age of moralizing tracts for children, this new book ventured out into new directions and offered to entertain adults as well as children. Its sales were staggering and its success rocketed Kate to fame and fortune. She now attracted a string of influential admirers, among them the most prestigious art critic of the time, John Ruskin, the popular medievalist painter Henry Stacy Marks, and the society dandy and poet Frederick Locker. Each had fallen under the Greenaway spell of innocence, and in time each would try to manipulate and control the progress and the life of its creator.

The Greenaway style was launched with *Under the Window* and perfected in her later books, including *Mother Goose*. It consisted of very personal almost childish preoccupations—the countryside, the past, idyllic settings of spring blossoms and pastel-tinted lanes, with young maidens in Regency dress and children in highly impractical long silken gowns walking down dusty country roads. The sun always shone in a Greenaway picture; the mobcaps and poke bonnets were worn for protection as well as effect. Hers is a world of childhood, where children walk decorously hand in hand, as well as taunt and tease, dance and cry. And yet each book suggests a darker, less joyful strain as well—the children in *Mother Goose* are occasionally lonely, Cross Patch waits bemused for her tea companion, Jumping Joan ponders how she is always alone. Such was the divided world of Kate Greenaway, a world that could both delight and disappoint, just as her own life had done.

For over ten years Kate Greenaway found herself typecast as the creator and high priestess of Victorian innocence, her books the ultimate in tasteful juvenilia. From 1878 to 1888 a plethora of annual Greenaway volumes appeared—books of nursery rhymes similar to *Mother Goose*, money-making productions such as the tiny almanacs and birthday books, a spelling book, as well as editions of children's stories by such popular authors as Charlotte Yonge and Bret Harte, embellished with Kate's illustrations. Their success inspired copyists, encouraged by the relentless commercialism of competitive publishers. Gradually, the pervasiveness of the Greenaway style and the fickle nature of the public forced Kate to reassess her position as an illustrator. Frustration and anger over her fading popularity and the misuse of her talent turned her bitter and reclusive, and by 1890 she had almost entirely abandoned illustration. Her career had lasted for a successful decade and provided her with the trappings of prosperity—a large house in Hampstead, designed by Norman Shaw, for herself and her family, a house with servants, which attested to her ability to support her aging parents. Her fame was well established; her name had become a household word.

Unfortunately, the final years of her life were lived far from the idyllic and enviable world pictured in many of her drawings. Having given up plans for more books, she turned instead to painting saleable pictures for the London galleries, landscapes with familiar figures and cottage scenes taken from excursions with her friend Helen Allingham. Most of these failed to sell, and that disappointment was coupled with a series of severe domestic tragedies which left her helpless and alone. When her beloved parents died, her will seemed to expire with them.

Throughout her career, the pervasive influence of the dictatorial John Ruskin left an emotional scar from which she would never recover. His effusive admiration of her "girlies," as he called her children, was aimed to gain her affection and obedience to his many time-consuming directives, and for over twenty years Kate submitted to his will, despite the sacrifice of valuable time. She had fallen in love with Ruskin, by then a sad, tired, aging giant given to fits of madness and irrational behavior which left Kate confused and ultimately heartbroken. A devoted disciple usually kept at bay by his rigid insistence that she work only for him, Kate pleaded for affection, which was rarely expressed. This one-sided love affair dominated her later career and seriously curtailed her output. It ended with Ruskin's death in 1900, leaving Kate stunned. She died the following year, a sad, slightly bitter woman, a victim, some might say, of her own innocence. She was then aged just fifty-five.

The Greenaway Vogue

"I really feel quite cross as I look at the shop windows and see the imitation books. It feels so queer, somehow, to see your ideas taken by someone else and put forth as theirs," Kate lamented to her mentor and sometime editor, Frederick Locker less than a year after her *Under the Window* triumph. Despite the encouragement and efforts of her many admirers, there was very little she could do to curtail such plagiarism. The Greenaway style was just too popular: it inspired not only complete pirated editions of her books, especially in America, but also such diverse items as Royal Doulton porcelain figures of Greenaway characters, jewelry, children's clothing, dolls, decorative doilies and needlework patterns of figures taken from her books, wallpaper inspired by her almanacs (one of the few authorized spinoffs), Greenaway soaps, perfumes, tonics, watches, and trade cards with Greenaway children extolling the virtues of such curiously disparate wares as pianos and sweets. Each of these items was stamped with Kate's trademark —the Greenaway child of an uncertain age and impish bearing, dressed in period costume with upturned nose, perfect round eyes, and a delicacy borrowed from the artist's careful study of Gainsborough's and Reynolds' child portraits. Its influence was indeed considerable. In a time of rather staid though occasionally garish taste, of dark cluttered rooms and heavy furniture, the pastel-colored world of the Greenaway child in all its simplicity swept into the nurseries and drawing rooms of the middle class. Kate's books were studied and copied by the most unsuspecting rivals: the young

Aubrey Beardsley, for example, creator of the decadent nineties' most scandalous images, had begun his career copying Greenaway children onto menu cards; later, he wrote his outrageous novel *Under the Hill*, inspired by Kate's *Under the Window* and the old woman who lived under the hill in Kate's *Mother Goose*.

The inspiration for the Greenaway style came from Kate's own innocent view of life around her. Once she asked a friend, who was bemused by her naiveté, "What do you think, is it not a beautiful world? . . . Have I got a defective faculty that few things are ugly to me?" It was just this degree of innocence that captivated generations of parents and children not only in Britain but also in America, on the Continent, and later in the Far East. Her books were lovingly read and carefully preserved—it is not uncommon to find a pristine copy of *Under the Window* even today. She charmed the children of the rich and the famous as well: her favorite London department store, Liberty, launched a line of Greenaway children's clothes, which were worn by the flamboyant dancer Isadora Duncan when she was a child, while the German kaiser, too, was dressed in Greenaway clothes as a little boy. Her books were soon translated into French, German, the Scandinavian languages, and Dutch, and her sales on the Continent were quite remarkable.

The Greenaway innocence could take rather an odd turn, however, as in the case of John Ruskin's misguided hold over Kate's work as it developed into book form. In one instance he urged her to abandon her real talent for costume figures and attempt some child nudes: "As we've got so far as taking off the hats, I trust we may in time get to take off just a little more—say mittens—and then—perhaps—even shoes! and—(for fairies) even . . . stockings—and then—." Later, her mistrust of her public and the relentless imitators turned her innocent view of life into a private crusade aimed at securing Ruskin's affection. This was the time she gave up illustration for gallery painting, when, throughout the 1890s, she invited child models to her studio in order to paint them in watercolors and oil. Neither medium seemed to be successful, and when such works appeared in the galleries they were generally dismissed as repetitive or weak imitations of more successful painters.

Nevertheless, the Greenaway vogue continued long after Kate gave up illustration. By the turn of the century, Greenaway fashions were still popular, while in 1946, her centenary year, among the laudatory articles were several intended to revive Greenaway fashions. By then a number of collectors of her books and paintings had joined the ranks of the antique hunters to pay high prices for Greenaway items.

Mother Goose

Kate Greenaway's *Mother Goose* was one of her most troublesome books to produce. Following on the heels of the astonishing success of *Under the Window*, it clearly helped to secure her position as one of the most popular book illustrators of her day. With all its innocent charm, it still had the same strong commercial appeal that *Under the Window* had demonstrated so brilliantly. Kate left the marketing of her books to her business manager, the master engraver and color printer Edmund Evans, and his publisher-associate George Routledge. Together they had seen the potential in her work and, after producing *Under the Window* in 1879, followed it the next year with her first precious giftbook, *Kate Greenaway's Birthday Book for Children*.

Kate quickly learned to keep several small sketchbooks filled with ideas for illustrations and books, brief pencil drawings, snatches of verse, settings she felt might be used in future drawings. However, Edmund Evans had the upper hand when it came to deciding which projects should be turned into books and, indeed, how they should be produced. A shrewd businessman with a keen eye for talent, Evans had earlier discovered and promoted the illustrations of Walter Crane. His series of *Mother Goose*–inspired nursery rhyme books such as *The Baby's Opera* and *Baby's Bouquet* proved remarkably popular when they were launched in Evans' series of nursery toybooks. Later, the young Randolph Caldecott joined forces with Evans to create his own highly successful series of colored nursery toybook illustrations. In time Crane, Caldecott, and Greenaway would capture the lucrative toybook market and be linked in their public's minds with some of the finest color-printed books for children ever produced.

It was in light of these past successes that Evans now proposed a nursery rhyme volume to follow *Kate Greenaway's Birthday Book for Children*.

Kate selected about fifty favorite Mother Goose rhymes, then very popular in Victorian nurseries, finally cutting the number down to forty-four. These she studied carefully, altering ever so slightly their traditional rhymes and rhythms to help with her illustrations. For example, in "Hark Hark" the traditional "velvet" is altered to "silken"; in "To Market" she alters "Market is done" to "Market is late"; while in "Elsie Marley" she alters "serve" to "feed." The result is not unlike her own rather halting, simple verses in *Under the Window*. In fact, Kate longed to be recognized for her poetic skills; she was a devoted follower of the famous poets of her day and numbered some of the most prominent Victorian poets among her acquaintances.

At the same time, she worked away at the illustrations with a characteristic thoroughness which, no doubt, she hoped her public would appreciate. First she produced brief pencil sketches built around a variety of ideas, either taken from the verses or from favorite images, groupings of children, or costumes that she designed. The themes she chose reveal her love of the countryside, country cottages, and landscapes borrowed from childhood memories of Nottinghamshire, as well as an occasional tasteful Aesthetic Movement element, such as the peacock feathers and blue-and-white china in "Cross Patch." Here, too, were the carefully trimmed box hedges and knot garden borders which suggest visits to Hampton Court, as well as skillful groupings of street urchins to recall her own Islington neighborhood· From these preliminary sketches she attempted watercolor illustrations done to size. Some were meticulously finished, like those in the sketchbooks reproduced here; others were only rough guides, while at least once she expanded a full-page illustration into a larger, complete watercolor, presumably as a gift for a friend.

A close examination of the marginal notes in this manuscript version of *Mother Goose* reveals just how seriously Kate Greenaway took her task. In one note she hints at the criticism Stacy Marks leveled against *Under the Window*—that she naively indicated shadows with long triangular blocks of black beneath each figure. Here she tells herself, "Try and show shadows by color and no black lines underneath." She was, in fact, her own fiercest critic, as these notes indicate: on the page for "To Market," after meticulously drawing a figure, she dislikes the effect and notes, "Find better background." On "Little Jack Horner," she suggests it would be better to "do without background" or even "move boy to side." A green clapboard house with its striking balcony was planned as a suitable background for "Lucy Lockett" but was not used in the final version. It was inspired by a house she had evidently studied while visiting the Suffolk seaside town of Lowestoft, as she notes in the margin.

Slowly and with great care the book took shape as Kate ruthlessly cut and altered ideas. One suspects the voice of her domineering mentor, John Ruskin, lay behind the choice of many of the images, since Kate was by this time well aware that he would pass judgment on her book. Moreover, she had placed herself in a position of extreme pressure not only to complete the book to deadline, but to maintain the high standards demanded of her by her public. Her worst fears were to be accused of repetition and laziness, as she notes alongside "Ring a Roses"—"Is this too much like Birthday Book?"

Over the past four years she had been groomed by Edmund Evans as an illustrator for color wood engravings. He demanded clarity, concise line, and accurate coloring, and she complied, adapting to this new technique just as she had learned, after considerable struggles, to design for the color lithographic printing of her greeting card designs. Her pastel tints and fine watercolor washes were even more amenable to wood engraving, and she carefully devised a color guide with marginal notes to indicate the exact color schemes she recommended. Color was, after all, an essential quality of her work, and from the earliest stages of her designs she kept the coloring in mind. At one point, her study of medieval manuscripts inspired the idea that the Mother Goose verses might be introduced with illuminated letters, as she noted, "Colour letters to begin verses." On favorite pages she prepared more finished designs, marking in watercolor the figure, the border, and in some instances the verses painted in with her fine brush. By now aware that the cover of her books helped sales, she took great care with *Mother Goose* and proposed a variety of binding cloth designs: one idea was for a trellis pattern "in green and blue linen," which was eventually altered to green and brown on white cloth in the published edition.

Once her preliminary dummy was completed, with watercolor pages and layouts clearly indicated, she sent it on to Evans for engraving. The technical process of wood engraving had developed greatly during this period, and the early crude black-and-white images found in newspapers and magazines now gave way to superbly cut and printed wood engravings. The process was laborious and involved a number of apprentices to cut the boxwood blocks to page size, plane them, transfer the drawing onto the surface, cut away the wood around each line, and then ink the block for printing. Kate learned these steps from her father, and this surely helped her to understand the amount of skill necessary to reproduce her watercolor sketches from wood blocks.

The color wood engraving was produced essentially the same way as the black-and-white, except that four individual blocks were needed, one for each color: a black (or occasionally brown) outline block contained the bare outline, a blue block was engraved only with those areas intended to reproduce blue, another for red, and another for yellow. These were combined to recreate the subtle pastel tones so important to the Greenaway style. Evans was also a master at mixing his own printer's inks and possessed a keen eye, which helped to interpret the amount of color necessary to allow the whiteness of the paper to temper and soften the finished engraved tones. It was standard policy for all of Evans' artists to receive color proofs for comment. In the case of *Mother Goose*, however, it was not permitted. Perhaps Kate had already spent too much time perfecting her drawings. She also insisted that the book be treated as a small, precious, almost antiquarian object, to be printed on textured paper of a quality and finish that dismayed Evans. Technically challenging, the printing of fine line and intricate tone on heavy paper at first seemed impossible to Evans. Yet he devised a method by which the rough textured paper was first pressed smooth through a series of copper plates which allowed for flat pages to be printed; thereafter, the paper's texture was restored by immersing each sheet in water to give a moderate yet acceptable appearance of age to the book. The rush to complete printing also affected the proofreading: among the typographical errors are an upturned "m" on page 25 of "Willy boy, Willy boy . . . if I may," and the trellis pattern cover with the "G" on Goose upside down.

It soon became clear to Kate that her hopes for *Mother Goose* had to be tempered. She sent out her first presentation copies to friends by September 1881, and their reactions merely confirmed her worst doubts. Frederick Locker, the poet, was surprised to find a recurrence of the melancholic sentiments that had cast their shadow on *Under the Window*, a cheerlessness which he felt marred her joyful, innocent style. He urged her to study the children painted by Romney and Reynolds and work hard next time to improve the expressions on her characters: "I do not think it would suit the style and spirit of your pictures if they were exactly *gay* children. But you must make your faces *happy*," he implored her. Locker was also appalled by the poor printing, the deep color, and sloppy overlapping of tones, which destroyed the essential outline and crisp clarity of her style. Kate could only nod in agreement and apologize to her patron on behalf of her printer: "The deep colour which you complain of in some is due to hurry, I'm afraid. There was no time to prove this book, and I never had any proof for correction at all, for Mr Evans said it was impossible, it must go; and some of the darker ones suffer in consequence. I know you imagine I'm always having them for correction, and sending them back and back again; but that is not so . . ." She assured him that her original intentions and hours spent carefully planning the book had been almost wasted. She had tried to practice what Ruskin had told her about color—that strong, bold color ("bright, happy color") was to be her goal—and this had unfortunately clouded her sense of delicacy; she was more anxious to create "a drawing which for colour is—is—too—too—as I look at it I feel happy." To convince Locker she was not totally at fault, she presented him with her original sketchbooks. These he lovingly preserved in a red morocco case in his famous Rowfant Library, and they are reproduced here complete for the first time, a family heirloom prefaced by the sentiments of Locker's daughter that they ought to be made accessible to a general public for "it is a pity for them to hide their beauty in the narrow little case."

Stacy Marks received his presentation copy in October and his response was more encouraging. He wrote to reassure her how much *Mother Goose* confirmed his belief in her abilities as a unique artist: "Your work always gives me pleasure—it seems so happy and so fearless of all the conventional rules and ideas that obtain generally about the art." He pointed out her more glaring errors, page by page, with a characteristic frankness that she relished: "Where, even in England, do you see such cabbagy trees? . . . How about a centre of gravity, madam? . . . You know I am conventional, but I am troubled to know why you don't make the hero of your story more conspicuous . . . As instance of fearlessness, I admire the pluck which can place a face directly against a window with each pane made out." If this was too severe, he concluded: "There! now I have finished, but I don't apologize for telling you the truth from my point of view, because I know you are strong enough to bear it and amiable enough to like it."

Although *Mother Goose* was not as successful commercially as the *Birthday Book* or *Under the Window*, it was a critical success. Kate received £252 for the use of her drawings, and eventually she earned £650 in royalties (compared with over £1500 for *Under the Window*). The critical reception was gratifying, and many thought the book surpassed *Under the Window* in charm and invention. The prestigious *Magazine of Art* called it "one of the prettiest, quaintest, most engaging little books imaginable." Kate Greenaway had proven herself and confirmed her role as the "fairy godmother" and creator of childish innocence: "If Miss Greenaway had done no more than *Mother Goose*, she would yet have done enough. Her place among nursery superstitions will be an honourable and good one for many and many a year."

At the same time, a second Greenaway book also appeared, the larger, rather overproduced *A Day in a Child's Life*, which proved a commercial failure. It was a chilling hint at the fickleness of fame and the danger of depending too much upon formulas. *The Times* critic offered a perceptive reason why the Greenaway vogue might not be as fresh and appealing as it first seemed and why the calculated prettiness of the books might not survive: "Miss Greenaway seems to be lapsing into a rather lackadaisical prettiness of style," the critic warned. It was in fact quite true, for the Greenaway vogue reached its height with the publication of *Mother Goose*.

Kate had to wait some time before John Ruskin offered his judgment on the book. He had recently recovered from another bout of madness, after being sent into a period of terrifying "blackness," which left him crushed and very much in need of solace. This he found in *Mother Goose*, especially in Kate's ability to recreate for him the memories of a lost innocence and his love for a "child-beauty" named Rose La Touche. Ruskin wrote how Kate's title page, with its provocative basket of roses and sleeping infant, immediately "struck his fancy" (Volume 2 of Notebooks). Not surprisingly, given his fragile mental state, Ruskin was not more forthcoming about *Mother Goose*. But the fact that the influential critic had responded positively gave Kate hope for her next book, and she set to work to create what was one of her most successful volumes, the classic *Little Ann*.

From the point of view of production, *Mother Goose* was one of the most elaborate and saleable of Greenaway's books. At least three separate first editions are known, bound in a variety of styles to entice the bookbuyer: there is an edition with glazed yellow paper board and a color illustration of a girl in a pink dress mounted on front and back covers; there is a turquoise blue and gilt stamped cloth binding; a white cloth edition with green and brown trellis design; as well as an "Author's Edition" bound in pink glazed boards with a painting of a mother and child on the front. The book was pirated in America in 1882 by the chief perpetrator of pirated Greenaway editions, McLoughlin Brothers, who were apparently so successful that they reissued extracts from *Mother Goose*, such as *Jack and Jill and Other Rhymes*, as separate books. The interest on the Continent quickly led to large sales of a German edition, *Ringel, Ringel, Reihe!*, and a French edition, *Scènes Familières*. Moreover, the original Routledge edition remained in print throughout the nineteenth century and continues in print today. As *Under the Window* had done, the book also sparked a remarkable miscellany of by-products, including Mother Goose stationery, needlework patterns, and greeting and trade cards. It had clearly helped to establish the Greenaway artistic style and it reinforced her position as a competent and talented artist. Her colleague Walter Crane was impressed enough with *Mother Goose* to include a reproduction from it in his pioneering study *Of the Decorative Illustration of Books*, 1897.

The original watercolor drawings, reproduced here in facsimile for the first time, are a telling reminder of Kate Greenaway's skills with the water-color brush. Her understanding of detail, her sense of line and delicate wash were unrivaled in her day. They have influenced generations of great children's illustrators, including Arthur Rackham and Beatrix Potter. A true miniaturist, she chose the delicate, the fine, and the pure from a world largely of her own creation and brought that world to life in words and images. This artless and unique work remains, in the following pages, as fresh as the day it was created—that indeed is the strength of the Greenaway magic.

London 1987

SKETCHBOOK I

Mother Goose
Vol. 1.
Given to F Locker
by Kate Greenaway
1882

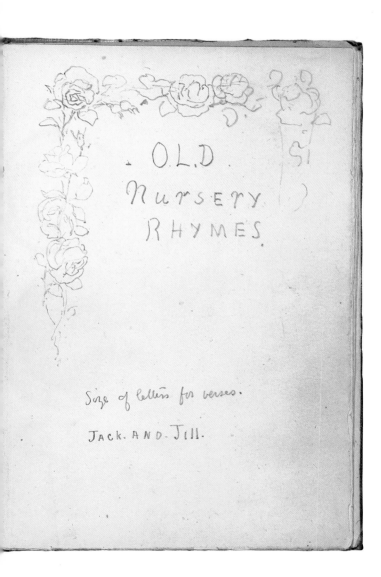

.O.L.D.

Nursery

RHYMES

Size of letters for verses.

Jack. AND. Jill.

Tell-Tale Tit,
Your tongue shall be slit
Aand all the Dogs in the Town
Shall hone a little bit

Tell-Tale Tit,
Your tongue shall be slit;
And all the dogs in the town
Shall have a little bit.

Oh, dear, what can the matter be?
Two old women
        got up in an apple tree.
One came down,
The other stayed till Saturday.

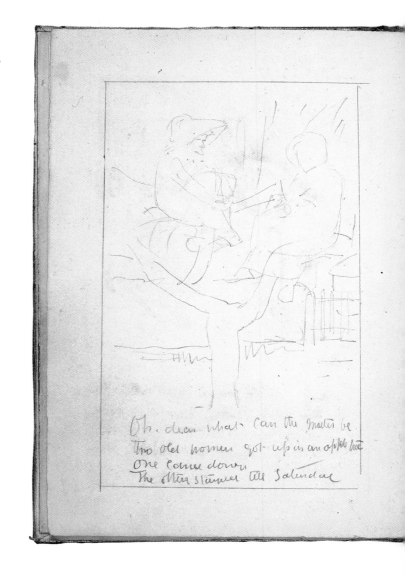

There was an old woman
    called nothing at all,
Who lives in a dwelling
    exceedingly small,
A man stretches his mouth to its
    utmost extent
And down at one gulp, home and
    old woman went.

Georgie Peorgie, pudding and pie,
Kissed the girls and made them cry;
When the girls begin to play,
Georgie Peorgie runs away.

Billy boy blue.
Come blow me your horn.
Your Sheep's in the meadow
Your Cow's in the Corn.
Is that the way you mind your sheep
Under the haycock. fast asleep.

Billy boy blue,
Come blow me your horn,
Your sheep's in the meadow,
Your cow's in the corn;
Is that the way you mind your sheep,
Under the haycock fast asleep?

Jack and Jill
Went up a hill,
To fetch a pail of water;
Jack fell down
And broke his crown,
And Jill came
Tumbling after.

As I was going up Pippin Hill

As I was going up Pippin Hill,
Pippin Hill was dirty;
There I met a sweet pretty lass,
And she dropped me a curtsey.

Bonny lass, pretty lass,
    wilt thou be mine?
Thou shalt not wash dishes,
Nor yet serve the swine;
Thou shalt sit on a cushion,
    and sew up a seam,
And thou shalt eat strawberries,
    sugar, and cream!

See Saw.

See-Saw-Jack in the hedge,
Which is the way to London Bridge?

To market, to market,
        to buy a plum cake,
Back again, back again,
        baby is late;
To market, to market,
        to buy a plum bun,
Back again, back again,
        market is done.

All around the green gravel,
The grass grows so green,
And all the pretty maids
    are fit to be seen;
Wash them in milk,
Dress them in silk,
And the first to go down
    shall be married.

Little Miss Muffet,
Sat on a tuffet,
Eating some curds and whey;
There came a great spider,
And sat down beside her,
And frightened Miss Muffet away.

Little Miss Muffet—

Willy boy, Willy boy, where are you going?
May I come with you, Yes if you may;
I'm going to the meadow to see them a mowing,
I'm going to help them make the Hay;

Willy boy, Willy boy,
    where are you going?
May I come with you,
Yes if you may;
I'm going to the meadow to see them
    a mowing,
I'm going to help them make the hay.

Girls and boys come out to play,
The moon it shines as bright as day;
Leave your supper,
    and leave your sleep,
And come to your playmates
    in the street;
Come with a whoop, come with a call,
Come with a good will,
    or come not at all;
Up the ladder and down the wall,
A halfpenny loaf will serve us all.

Girls and boys, Come out to play.

Gray goose and gander,
Waft your wings together,
And carry the good King's daughter
Over the one Strand River.

There was a little man, and he
lived by himself
And all the breads and cheese he got
He put upon a shelf.
But the rats and the mice they
made so much strife
He was forced to go to London
to buy a little wife
The streets were so crowded and the
lanes were so narrow,
He was forced to bring his little wife
Home in a barrow.

There was a little man, and he lived by himself
And all the bread and cheese he got
He put upon a shelf.
But the rats and the mice they made so much strife
He was forced to go to London, to buy a little wife
The Streets were so crowd, and the lanes were so narrow,
He was forced to bring his little wife
Home in a barrow.

Jack Sprat could eat no fat,
His wife could eat no lean;
And so betwixt them both,
They licked the platter clean.

Little maid, little maid,
Whither goest thou?
Down in the meadow
To milk my cow.

"Little maid, Pretty maid, Whither goest thou?"
"Down in the Meadows to milk my Cow."

As Tommy Snooks, and Bessie Brooks
Were walking out one Sunday;
Says Tommy Snooks to Bessie Brooks,
"To-morrow—will be Monday."

Rock-a-bye baby,
Thy cradle is green;
Father's a nobleman,
Mother's a queen.
And Betty's a lady,
And wears a gold ring;
And Johnny's a drummer,
And drums for the king.

Rock-a-bye baby thy cradle is green;
Father's a nobleman, mother's a queen.
And Betty's a lady, and wears a gold ring,
And Johnny a drummer, and drums for the king

Here am I, little Jumping Joan,
Where nobodys with me,
I'm always alone.

Here am I, little jumping Joan,
When nobody's with me,
I'm always alone.

My mother and your mother,
Went over the way;
Said your mother to my mother,
"It's chop-a-nose day."

My Mother and Your Mother
Went over the way.
Said your mother to my mother
Its Chop-a nose day.

Figures more in middle.

Elsie Marley has grown so fine,
She won't get up to serve the swine;
But lies in bed till eight or nine.
And surely she does take her time.

Little Jack Horner sat in the corner,
Eating a Christmas pie;
He put in his thumb,
    and pulled out a plum,
And said, oh! what a good boy am I.

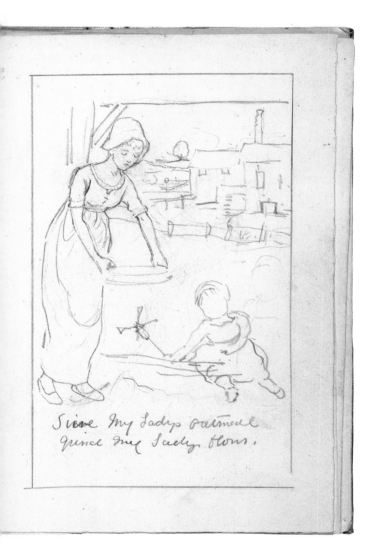

Sieve my lady's oatmeal
Grind my lady's flour.

Sieve my lady's oatmeal
Grind my lady's flour.

49

Goosey, goosey, gander,
Where shall I wander?
Up stairs, down stairs,
And in my lady's chamber:
There I met an old man,
Who would not say his prayers;
Take him by the left leg,
Throw him down the stairs.

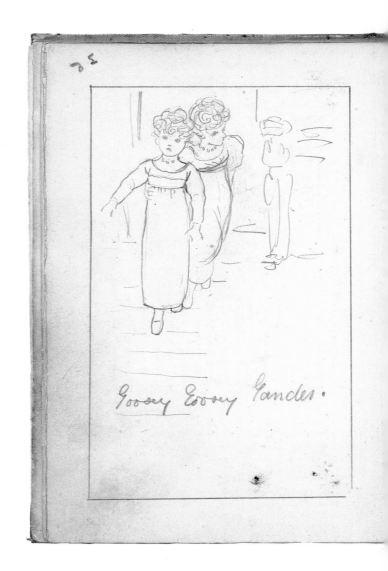

Goosey Goosey Gander.

Cross Patch, lift the latch

Cross Patch, lift the latch,
Sit by the fire and spin;
Take a cup, and drink it up,
Then call your neighbours in.

Draw a pail of water,
For my lady's daughter;
My father's a king, and my
mother's a queen,
My two little sisters
are dressed in green,
Stamping grass and parsley,
Marigold leaves and daisies.
One rush! two rush!
Pray thee, fine lady,
come under my bush.

As I was going up Pippin Hill

As I was going up Pippin Hill,
Pippin Hill was dirty;
There I met a sweet pretty lass,
And she dropped me a curtsey.

As I was going up Pippin Hill,
Pippin Hill was dirty;
There I met a sweet pretty lass,
And she dropped me a curtsey.

As I was going up Pippin Hill
Pippin Hill was dirty
There I met a sweet pretty lass
And she dropped me a curtsey.

Goosey, goosey, gander,
Where shall I wander?
Up stairs, down stairs,
And in my lady's chamber:
There I met an old man,
Who would not say his prayers;
Take him by the left leg,
Throw him down the stairs.

Little Miss Muffet,
Sat on a tuffet,
Eating some curds and whey;
There came a great spider,
And sat down beside her,
And frightened Miss Muffet away.

We're all jolly boys, and we're coming
        with a noise,
Our stockings shall be made
Of the finest silk,
And our tails shall trail the ground.

Tom Tom. The Piper's Son.

Tom, Tom, the Pipers Son,
He learnt to play when he was young.

Tom, Tom, the piper's son,
He learnt to play when he was young,
He with his pipe made such a noise,
That he pleased all the girls and boys.

Lucy Locket, lost her pocket,
Kitty Fisher found it;
There was not a penny in it,
But a ribbon round it.

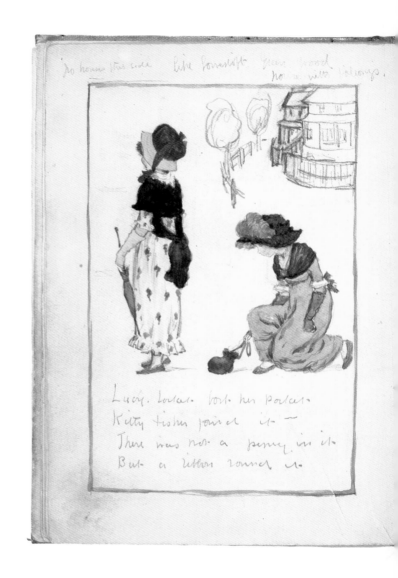

Ring a Ring a. Roses.
A Pocket full of posies
Hush. hush. Hush hush.
We're all tumbled down

Ring-a-ring-a-roses,
A pocket full of posies;
Hush! hush! hush! hush!
We're all tumbled down.

61

Mary, Mary, quite contrary,
How does your garden grow?
With silver bells, and cockle shells,
And cowslips all of a row.

Polly put the kettle on,
Polly put the kettle on,
Polly put the kettle on,
We'll all have tea.
Sukey take it off again,
Sukey take it off again,
Sukey take it off again,
They're all gone away.

Hark! hark! the dogs bark,
The beggars are coming to town;
Some in rags and some in tags,
And some in cotton gowns.
Some gave them white bread,
And some gave them brown,
And some gave them
     a good horse-whip,
And sent them out of the town.

Little Tom Tucker,
Sang for his supper.
What did he sing for?
Why, white bread and butter.
How can I cut it without a knife?
How can I marry without a wife?

Humpty Dumpty sat on a wall,
Humpty Dumpty had a great fall.

There was an old woman
Lived under a hill;
And if she's not gone,
She lives there still.

Ride a cock-horse,
To Banbury-cross,
To see little Johnny
Get on a white horse.

SKETCHBOOK II

See Saw, Jack in the Hedge.
Where is the way to London Bridge.

See-Saw Jack in the hedge,
Which is the way to London Bridge?

One foot up, the other foot down,
That's the way to London town.

One foot up, the other foot down.
That's the way to London Town.

Little Bo-peep has lost her sheep,
And can't tell where to find them;
Leave them alone, and they'll come home,
And bring their tails behind them.

Little Tommy Tittlemouse,
Lived in a little house;
He caught fishes
In other men's ditches.

Little Tommy Little Mouse
lived in a little house.
He caught fishes
In other mens Ditches

Diddlty, diddlty, dumpty,
The cat ran up the plum tree;
Give her a plum, and down she'll come,
Diddlty, diddlty, dumpty.

NURSERY. RHYMES
7OR. CHILDREN.

Illustrated by.
KATE. GREENAWAY.

Engraved and printed
by.
Edmond. EVANS.

Daffy-down-dilly has come up to town,
In a yellow petticoat and a green gown.

Johnny shall have a new bonnet,
And Johnny shall go to the fair;
And Johnny shall have a blue ribbon,
To tie up his bonny brown hair.

Johnny shall have a new bonnet,
And Johnny shall go to the fair;
And Johnny shall have a blue ribbon,
To tie up his bonny brown hair.

There was a little boy and a little girl
Lived in an alley.
Says the little boy to the little girl
Shall I, oh, shall I.

But the children more on top of page.

There was a little boy and a little girl
Lived in an alley;
Says the little boy to the little girl,
"Shall I, oh, shall I?"
Says the little girl to the little boy,
"What shall we do?"
Says the little boy to the little girl,
"I will kiss you!"

Little Betty Blue,
Lost her holiday shoe.
What will Betty do?
Why, give her another,
To match the other,
And then she will walk in two.

A diller, a dollar,
A ten o'clock scholar;
What makes you come so soon?
You used to come at ten o'clock,
But now you come at noon!

Little boy, little boy,
Where wast thou born,
Far off in Lancashire
Under a thorn.
Where they sup sour
Milk in a ram's horn.

Little lad, little lad,
Where wast thou born?
Far off in Lancashire,
Under a thorn;
Where they sup sour
Milk from a ram's horn.

Little girl, little girl
Where have you been
Gathering roses,
To give to the Queen.

Little girl, little girl
Where have you been
Gathering roses,
To give to the Queen.

Cross Patch, lift the latch,

Sit by the fire and spin;

Take a cup, and drink it up,

Then call your neighbours in.

93

Hark! hark! the dogs bark,
The beggars are coming to town;
Some in rags and some in tags,
And some in cotton gowns.
Some gave them white bread,
And some gave them brown,
And some gave them a good horse-whip,
And sent them out of the town.